One of the Family

By Peggy Archer
Illustrated by Ruth Sanderson

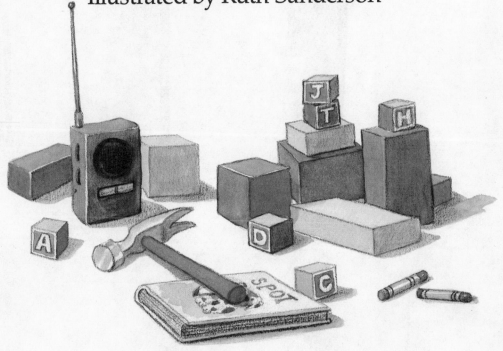

Golden Press • New York
Western Publishing Company, Inc., Racine, Wisconsin

Melissa was the Brown family's new baby.

Carrie liked having a little sister. When Mother
let her, Carrie rocked Melissa and sang to her.
"Rock-a-bye, baby..." But most of the time Melissa
was sleeping, so Carrie sang to her doll.

Bob liked reading. He tried to read to his new sister and show her the pictures in his books. But Melissa sighed and went on sleeping.

Zzaw, zzaw, went Davey's saw. "Look, Melissa," said Davey. "I'm making a birdhouse to hang in the big tree in the back yard. You'll be able to look out the window and see all the birds."
Melissa just kept on sleeping.

Craig liked to listen to music and dance. He thought the new baby was a little boring. But he kept an eye on Melissa, just to make sure no one bothered her too much.

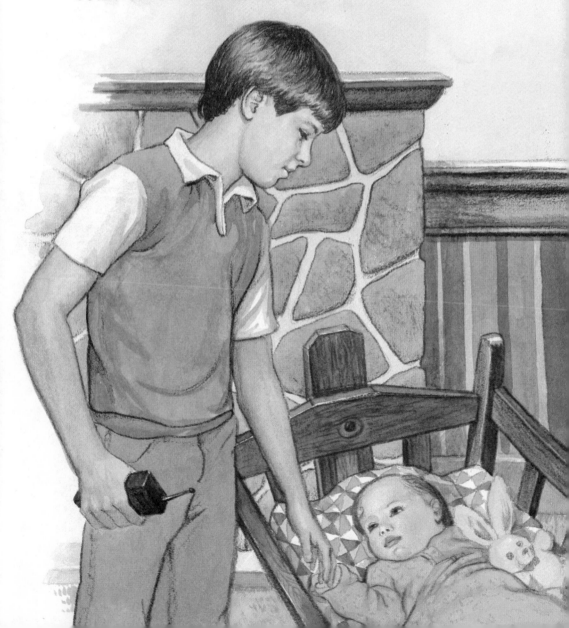

As the weeks went by, Melissa started to stay awake a little longer. Now when Carrie sang to her, Melissa stared with big, open eyes and kicked her feet.

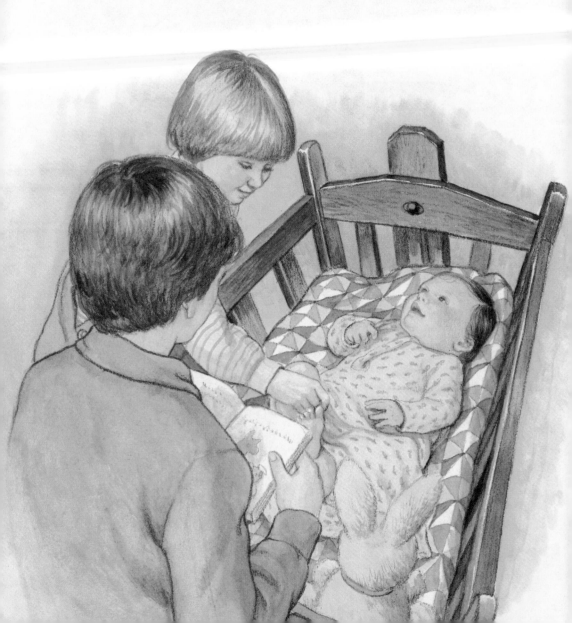

And when Craig danced, she followed his movements with her eyes. Once she even rolled over.

One day Mr. and Mrs. Brown decided to go out. Miss Webber, the babysitter, came to stay with the children.

Craig was listening to his favorite music on the radio and eating a peanut-butter sandwich.

Davey was making a tool caddy. *Bang, bang,* went his hammer.

Bob was copying pictures from a book he liked. Carrie was building a block tower and singing. "Old MacDonald had a farm..." *Crash!* went the blocks.

"Goodness, gracious!" said Miss Webber. "This house is much too noisy for a baby. Babies need peace and quiet so they can go to sleep."

Craig turned off the radio.

Davey stopped pounding and put down the hammer.

Carrie put the blocks away. "On his farm he had a pig," she sang. Melissa smiled and kicked. "Ssh!" everyone said to Carrie. She stopped singing.

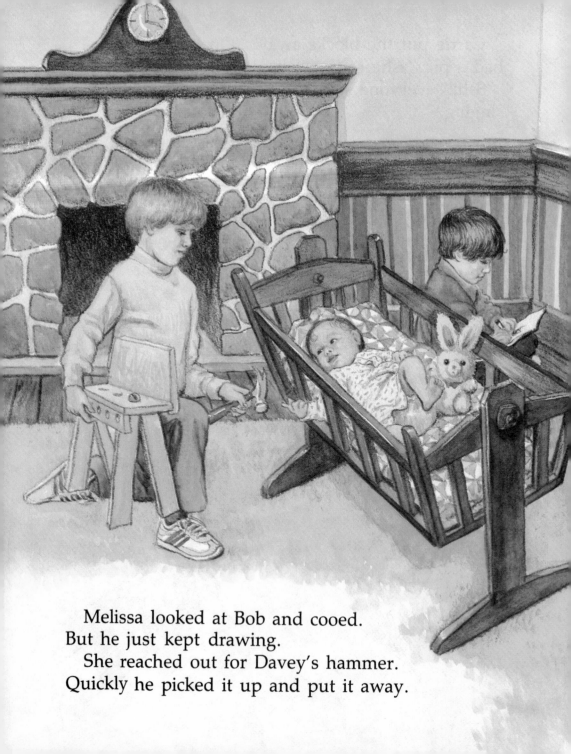

Melissa looked at Bob and cooed.
But he just kept drawing.
  She reached out for Davey's hammer.
Quickly he picked it up and put it away.

She looked at Craig, but all he
did was eat his sandwich.
"Waa!" Melissa began to cry.

"She likes to rock," Carrie said to Miss Webber.
So Miss Webber sat down in the rocker with
Melissa. Back and forth they rocked. But Melissa
didn't stop crying.

"Maybe she's hungry," Davey said.

Miss Webber tried to give Melissa a bottle, but she only cried harder.

"She's probably wet," said Craig. Miss Webber changed Melissa's diaper, but Melissa kept on crying.

"She likes it when I read to her," said Bob.
"And she likes my hammer," said Davey.
"And my music," added Craig.

Miss Webber thought for a moment. "Well," she said finally, "I suppose a little noise couldn't hurt."

Craig turned on his radio with the sound low.
He tapped his feet in time to the music.

Davey started working on the tool caddy again.
Bang, bang, went his hammer.

Bob showed Melissa the pictures he had drawn, and began reading her the story that went with them.

Carrie rebuilt her tower. *Crash!* went the blocks. "Old MacDonald had a farm," Carrie sang happily.

Melissa stopped crying. She smiled and cooed for a while. Soon her eyes closed halfway, then all the way, and she fell fast asleep.

Miss Webber smiled. "I can see that this is one baby who *doesn't* need peace and quiet," she said. "I guess Melissa is just one of the family."